Good Night, Mr. Night

dan yaccarino

Gulliver Books

Harcourt Brace & Company

San Diego   New York   London

Gulliver Books is a registered trademark of
Harcourt Brace & Company.

Library of Congress Cataloging-in-Publication Data
Yaccarino, Dan.
Good night, Mr. Night/Dan Yaccarino
[author and illustrator].
p. cm.
"Gulliver Books."
Summary: Mr. Night puts the world to bed and
helps children fall asleep.
ISBN 0-15-201319-9
[1. Night—Fiction. 2. Bedtime—Fiction.] I. Title.
PZ7.Y125Go 1997
[E]—dc20   96-25042

F E D C B

Printed in Singapore

The illustrations in this book were painted in
alkyds on Arches watercolor paper.
The display type was set in Univers Extended
Extra Black.
The text type was set in Univers Extended Black.
Color separations by Bright Arts, Ltd., Singapore
Printed and bound by Tien Wah Press, Singapore
This book was printed on totally chlorine-free
Nymolla Matte Art paper.
Production supervision by Stanley Redfern and
Pascha Gerlinger
Designed by Kaelin Chappell and Dan Yaccarino

For Dad

When the sun slowly falls
just over the hill, Mr. Night wakes.

Sometimes I can hear him walking the earth, brushing past the trees.

Mr. Night closes the flowers,

he quiets the animals,

and calms the sea.

Mr. Night keeps each star in its place.

When I see him at my window,
I know it's time for bed.

He gently closes my eyes and I fall fast asleep.

He whispers dreams to me

and plays music I hear only when I'm sleeping.

Then, when the sun starts to rise,
Mr. Night grows tired.

He lies down just over
the hill and drifts off to sleep.

And when I wake, I whisper,
"Good night, Mr. Night."